Tadpoles

Stroppy
Poppy

First published in 2006 by
Franklin Watts
338 Euston Road
London
NW1 3BH

Franklin Watts Australia
Hachette Children's Books
Level 17/207 Kent Street
Sydney
NSW 2000

Text © Sue Graves 2006
Illustration © Desideria Guicciardini 2006

A CIP catalogue record for this book is available
from the British Library.

ISBN (10) 0 7496 6543 2 (hbk)
ISBN (13) 978-0-7496-6543-2 (hbk)
ISBN (10) 0 7496 6893 8 (pbk)
ISBN (13) 978-0-7496-6893-8 (pbk)

Series Editor: Jackie Hamley
Series Advisor: Dr Hilary Minns
Series Designer: Peter Scoulding

Printed in China

Franklin Watts is a division
of Hachette Children's Books.

Stroppy Poppy

by Sue Graves

Illustrated by Desideria Guicciardini

W

FRANKLIN WATTS

LONDON • SYDNEY

Sue Graves

"Do you ever get stroppy like Poppy? It's not a very nice feeling, is it? Luckily, Poppy's much better behaved now and never gets stroppy at all!"

Desideria Guicciardini

"I was born in a castle in Florence in Italy. I like drawing angry ladies. I never eat puddings and I'm almost always in a good mood."

Poppy was
always cross.

Everyone called her Stroppy Poppy.

Mum asked her to dry the dishes.

Poppy got stroppy.

Dad asked her
to tidy her room.

Poppy got stroppy.

Granny asked her
to feed the dog.

Poppy got very stroppy!

Then everyone had
a good idea.

When Poppy asked everyone to play a game with her ...

... they all got stroppy!

Poppy was sorry.

Now Poppy's not stroppy any more!

Notes for adults

TADPOLES is structured to provide support for newly independent readers. The stories may also be used by adults for sharing with young children.

Starting to read alone can be daunting. **TADPOLES** helps by providing visual support and repeating words and phrases. These books will both develop confidence and encourage reading and rereading for pleasure.

If you are reading this book with a child, here are a few suggestions:

1. Make reading fun! Choose a time to read when you and the child are relaxed and have time to share the story.

2. Talk about the story before you start reading. Look at the cover and the blurb. What might the story be about? Why might the child like it?

3. Encourage the child to reread the story, and to retell the story in their own words, using the illustrations to remind them what has happened.

4. Discuss the story and see if the child can relate it to their own experience, or perhaps compare it to another story they know.

5. Give praise! Remember that small mistakes need not always be corrected.

If you enjoyed this book, why not try

another **TADPOLES** story?